# JAMPiRES

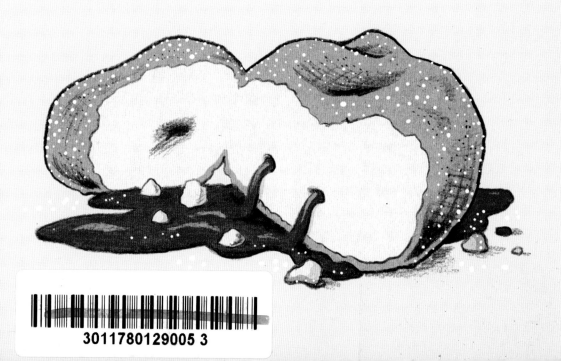

**MIX**
Paper from
responsible sources
**FSC® C104723**

FSC
www.fsc.org

Layout and lettering
designed by Ness Wood

Words edited by Alice Corrie

JAMPIRES
was written and illustrated by
Sarah McIntyre & David O'Connell
and is a A DAVID FICKLING BOOK

First published in Great Britain in 2014
by David Fickling Books.,
31 Beaumont Street,
Oxford, OX1 2NP

www.davidficklingbooks.com
www.jampires.com

Jam for breakfast,
Jam on bread,
Lunch and dinner,
Jam in bed.
Jampires slurp up Jam all day!
Jampires all say,
"JAM, HOORAY!"

# JAMPIRES

Sarah McIntyre    David O'Connell

For James and Treacle

David Fickling Books

www.jampires.com

So Sam set a trap
before going to bed
and used his dry doughnut as bait.

In place of the jam
he used ketchup instead,

then hid under the covers to **wait**.

In the dark he awoke to a **hullabaloo!**

First came

# Slurp!

And

Then

But what a surprise!
Was there **one** thief?
**No,**
**two!**

And their mouths
showed the glint of a
FANG!

And we both got SO hungry we couldn't resist
slurping from what we could find.
A dollop of jam would never be missed!
Or at least, we thought
you'd not mind."

"It's a deal", said Sam,
and took hold of their hands,
and they opened the window and flew . . .

...over rivers and oceans and strange distant lands,

and UP through the star-speckled blue.

And there in the sky, such a huge jar of JAM, with Jampires in flocks soaring by,

above doughnuts that looked plump as cushions to Sam, and mountains of blueberry pie . . .

Over fields full of jam tarts, growing like flowers, sprinkled with white sherbet snow,

and castles of sponge cake with gingerbread towers
lit up by the ice-cream moon's glow . . .

To skyberry orchards
where Jampire mums perched
under a sugar-frost dome.

With hoots of contentment the mums made a fuss.

They BURBLED and CHORTLED with joy.

So they thanked him with doughnuts, the jammiest kind, which they bring to his house every day.

And although they suspect that Sam wouldn't mind, they don't suck out the jam on the way!

"So where DO we find all the JAM we adore?

Well . . .